For Ste xx

OXFORD
UNIVERSITY PRESS

Great Clarendon Street, Oxford OX2 6DP

Oxford New York

Athens Auckland Bangkok Bogotá Buenos Aires Cape Town Chennai Dar es Salaam Delhi
Florence Hong Kong Istanbul Karachi Kolkata Kuala Lumpur Madrid Melbourne Mexico City
Mumbai Nairobi Paris São Paulo Singapore Taipei Tokyo Toronto Warsaw

with associated companies in Berlin Ibadan

Oxford is a registered trade mark of Oxford University Press
in the UK and in certain other countries

Copyright © Joanne Partis 2002

The moral rights of the author have been asserted

First published 2002

British Library Cataloguing in Publication Data available

ISBN 0–19–279073–0 (hardback)
ISBN 0–19–272485–1 (paperback)

1 3 5 7 9 10 8 6 4 2

Typeset in Postcard
Printed in Malaysia

Arnie...
the Accidental Hero

Joanne Partis

OXFORD

UNIVERSITY PRESS

Arnie the armadillo was not a brave animal. He liked flowers, and butterflies, and sunshine. But Arnie was nervous. Arnie was shy. And Arnie was scared of everything!

He was scared of snakes, and of water, of bats, and of thunderstorms.

But most of all Arnie was scared of crocodiles.

Even thinking about them made him shake.

One day Arnie was dozing in the
shade of a palm tree.
     Suddenly, all around there were
noisy thuds. Arnie was so frightened,
he rolled himself up into a ball.

Slowly, he uncurled himself. His friends
Parrot and Tortoise were laughing.
    'Arnie's scared of bananas,'
they giggled.

On the ground lay lots
of squashy bananas.

Arnie felt silly. He wished he wasn't
always so timid.
　　His friends ran off to the other
side of the island.
　　'Come and play with us—if you
dare!' they called.
　　Arnie didn't like being left behind.

I'll show them I can be brave, he thought. And, following their foot-prints, he set off into the jungle.
It wasn't scary at all until Arnie turned a corner and, *oh no* . . .

'Snakes!' said Arnie.
I can be brave, he thought.
He took a deep breath . . .

and tiptoed past the slippery snakes
as quietly as he could.
But just around the next corner,
oh no . . .

'Water!' said Arnie.
The river was deep and Arnie was frightened.
But he could still see the footprints on the
other side.

He took a deep breath and clambered carefully across a log.
But just then, the sky turned very dark.

'Thunder!' he shivered.
But Arnie was being brave. He took a deep
breath and ran through the storm.

Up ahead he could see
footprints leading into a
warm, dry cave.
He ran inside but,
oh no . . .

'Bats!' said Arnie. Lots of upside-down yellow eyes were watching him. He took a deep breath and scurried through as quickly as he could.

By now Arnie wasn't feeling
very brave at all.

He came out of the cave into the sun
and Arnie felt much better.
At last he could see his friends.

But then he saw something else as well.

A CROCODILE!
It was creeping up on Parrot and Tortoise.

Arnie was more afraid than he had
ever been of snakes or bats
or thunderstorms.
     But he knew he had
to warn his friends.

He started to run towards them. *Oh no!*
He was too close to the edge.
                    He tripped and . . .

whoosh!

He rolled off
and fell . . .

. . . down

. . . down

. . .down

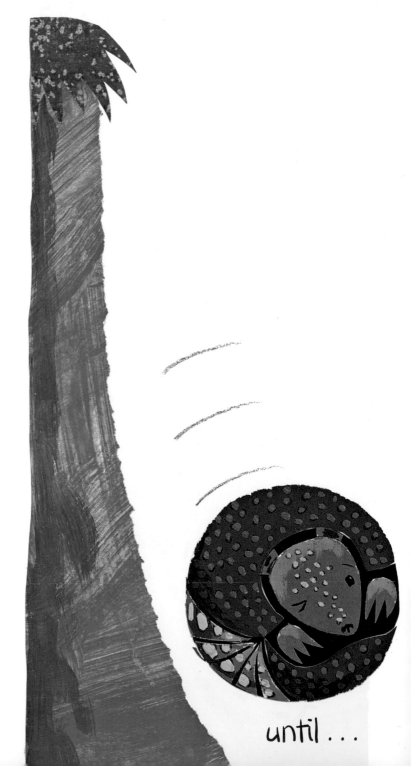

until . . .

Parrot and Tortoise cheered.
     'We're sorry we laughed at you,' they said.
  'We didn't know that you were so brave.'

'No,' said Arnie, rubbing his head.
'Neither did I.'